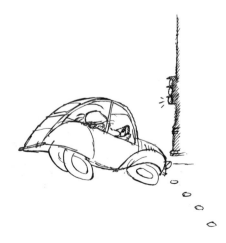

sempé

Nothing is Simple

Φ

George, I'm scared!

1.

3.

2.

4.

1.

2.

3.

1.

2.

5.

6.

3.

4.

7.

*We ought to ask the landlord if there isn't some other
way for the caretaker to make announcements.*

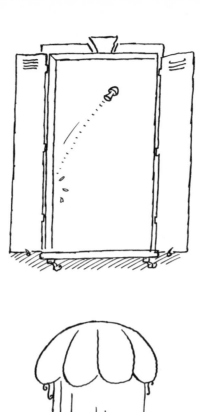

"It has just been reported that after the American delegate made his comment,
Mr Krushchev scratched his nose twice, a telling sign of his deep dissatisfaction!"

1.

2.

3.

4.

5.

6.

You're boring the doctor, Isabelle.

1.

2.

5.

6.

3.

4.

7.

8.

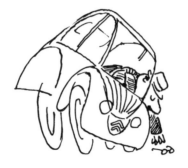

1.

2.

3.

4.

5.

6.

"And now let me ask you the question that all our viewers will be asking themselves: how does your oneiric concept, Kafkaesque as its basic tendency is, co-exist with the sublogical vision you entertain of intrinsic existence in itself?"

Sempé.

I've cut his part drastically, but he doesn't know about it yet.

1.

2.

5.

6.

9.

10.

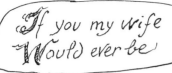

3.

4.

7.

8.

11.

12.

Man overboard! **MY** *man overboard!*

Shall we, Lucy?

1.

2.

3.

4.

And how's that lawsuit of yours going?

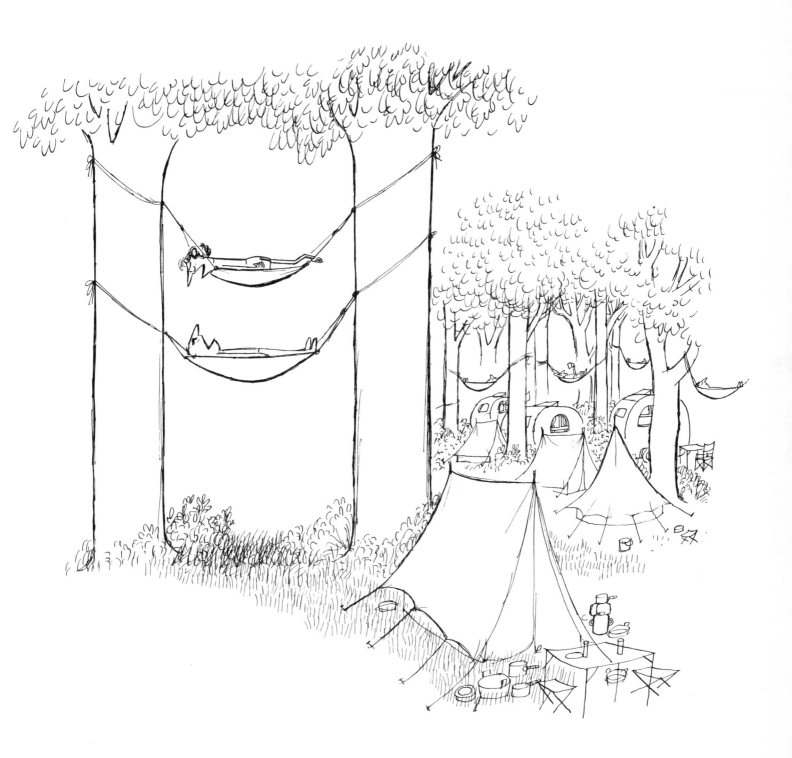

It keeps moving.

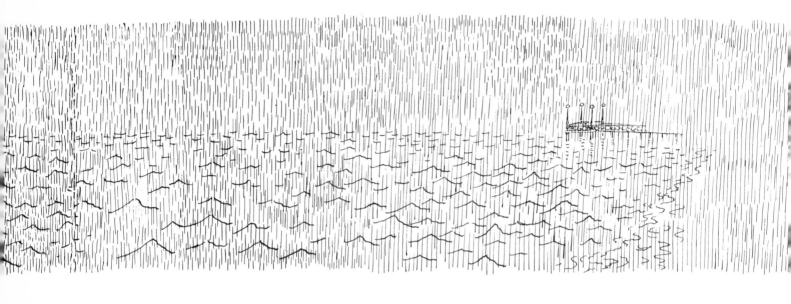

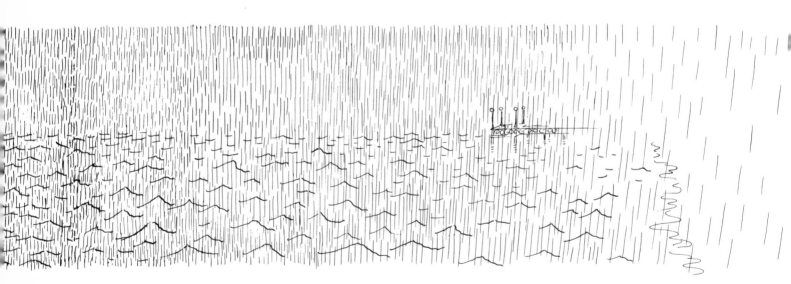

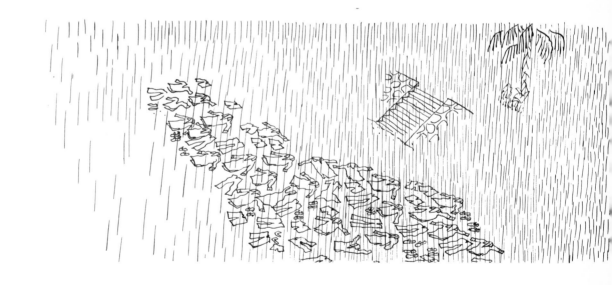

1.

3.

2.

4.

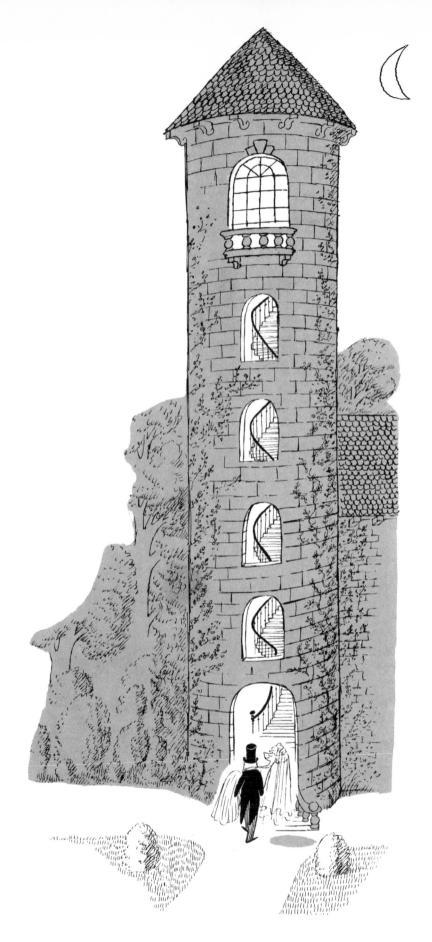

1.

2.

3.

1.

3.

2.

4.

Sempé

Friday 2nd
Mr Lambert had a visitor: a young woman, a platinum blonde.
We pretended not to notice, but you couldn't help seeing that she
wasn't wearing a wedding ring. (Mr Lambert was, though.)

Sunday 4th

Mr Cusinet went fishing this morning and fell into the rough sea. Mr Martineau, who happened to be passing, jumped in and pulled him out of the water. When we all told him how brave he'd been Mr Martineau was very modest, and said that anyone would have done the same in his place.

Tuesday 6th

After dinner we talked about Berlin, Bizerte and Picasso. Mr Martineau explained all sorts of things to us. When we started discussing Picasso, Mr Martineau (who knows him) told us that he really paints normally – like you or me – but then he cuts up his canvases to make them look peculiar, and he even sometimes paints blindfold, just to please his snobbish public. As Mr Cazenave said: when you know the real story you see that these people are just playing on human gullibility. Mr Cusinet was the only one who didn't agree with Mr Martineau's opinions, even though Mr Martineau saved him from drowning less than three days ago. That rather shocked us!

Friday 9th
Raining.
Lunch started off with Mr Marcellin launching into a couple of jokes which made everyone burst out laughing, and it looked as if we were going to have a fun afternoon. But then Mr Marcellin went quiet, as he obviously couldn't think of anything else to say, so we all went upstairs for a siesta.

Saturday 10th

Something happened at dinner this evening which rather reminded us of that time when Gina Lollobrigida and Liz Taylor met in Moscow: Mrs Thomas and Mrs Cazenave came down to dinner in the same dress. After the initial shock had passed, we discovered what had happened. They'd both bought the dress from their local dressmaker (one in Argentiers-sur-Orge and the other in Tournay), who had assured them both that it was an exclusive design. That doesn't bode well for the reputation of their local boutiques.

Sunday 11th
An electrifying incident heightened the edgy atmosphere of the last two days. We could really
have done without this! All the people who had ordered yoghurt got fromage frais instead,
and everyone who wanted fromage frais was served yoghurt …

Wednesday 14th

Although everything is very casual here, we dress more formally for dinner than for lunch.
But imagine how surprised we were to see Mr and Mrs Cazenave dressed to the nines!
As far as anyone could gather, they were celebrating their wedding anniversary. They drank
champagne and called each other darling. As Mrs Chapo said, it wasn't that we were
jealous, because after all, all the men here have their smart navy-blue suits at home and all the
women have their furs, but we did feel they were being rather ostentatious.

Saturday 17th
Twelve large trunks arrived this morning. Everyone was dressed with the utmost elegance
at dinner – except for the Cazenaves, who were in shorts and T-shirts.
We all looked really great, but as I mentioned before, the Cazenaves were in casual clothes.

Monday 19th
Mrs Allegro is so keen to show off her likeness to Brigitte Bardot that she insists on
copying the star's hairstyle. We're all amazed. Particularly since her children have been
very badly brought up, and it's obvious that she doesn't pay them enough attention.

Friday 23rd

Everyone here knows that Mr Chapo supports the Government and Mr Casenave supports the Opposition. So there was bound to be a political argument some time, but it went on so long that the women and children went to bed. Mr Thomas and Mr Marcillac acted as go-betweens, so, late at night, everyone came to an agreement (for as the barman remarked next day, men of goodwill can always find something to agree on), and Mr Laurent wrote a manifesto saying that liberty and full employment must be regarded as sacrosanct, and everyone who had joined in the argument signed it.

Tuesday 27th

Not content with saving Mr Cusinet's life, Mr Martineau decided to give him swimming lessons. He began by forbidding him to drink wine, and then (in spite of Mr Cusinet's protests) he said he mustn't smoke either! And then, when Mr Martineau found him smoking this morning, Mr Cusinet lost his temper. He made us all go to the scene of the life-saving incident and jumped into the water, to show that he could have come up on his own perfectly well without any help from Mr Martineau. Then he made a point of standing right by Mr Martineau, with a cigarette in his mouth. Mr Martineau just ignored him and went on reading the paper.

Friday 30th

Almost everyone is leaving. We've all exchanged addresses and promised to keep in touch. As Mr Martineau was about to leave, his car looked as if it might break down, but Mr Cusinet, who is staying another two days, helped him to get it on the road.

Martha, my love, is it all right if I go hunting?

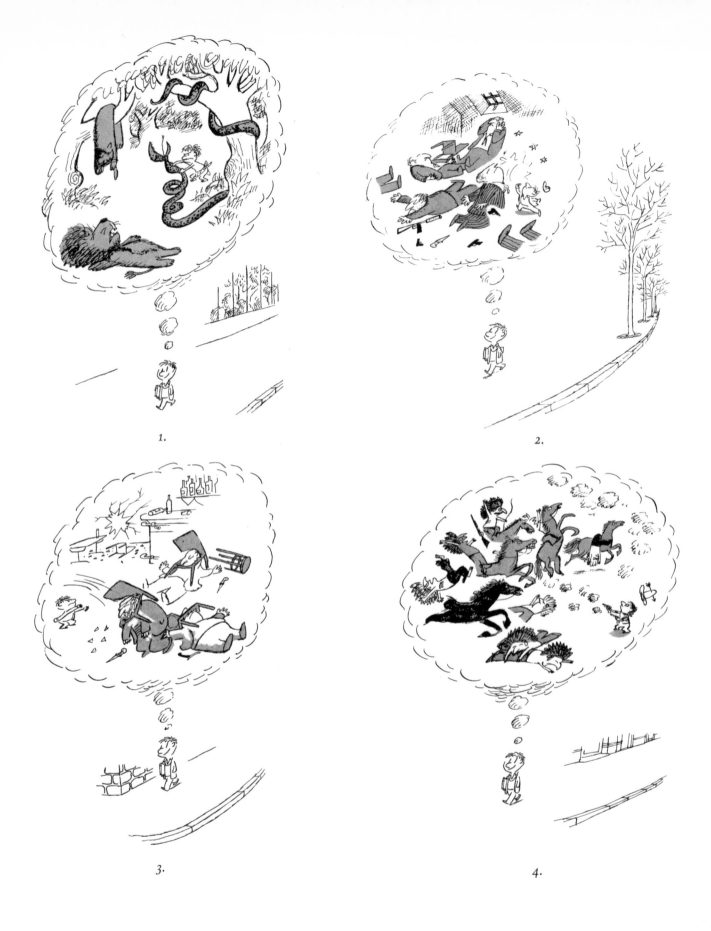

1.

2.

3.

4.

5.

6.

Sempé

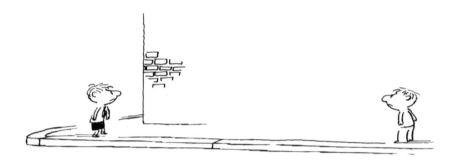

1.

4.

2.

3.

5.

6.

8.

7.

9.

Your father and I have to go away. Promise to be bad.

False alarm! They're just delivering the battering ram I ordered last week.

So just why didn't you perform the manoeuvre, Mr Martin ?

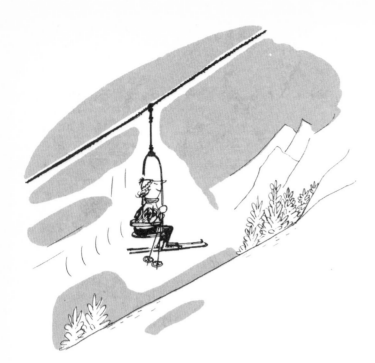

1.

2.

5.

6.

3.

4.

7.

1.

3.

2.

4.

Still, the owners will be glad we managed
to save part of the cargo!

1.

2.

3.

4.

5.

6.

7.

8.

9.

10.

11.

Phaidon Press Limited
Regent's Wharf
All Saints Street
London N1 9PA

Phaidon Press Inc.
180 Varick Street
New York, NY 10014

www.phaidon.com

English Edition © 2006 Phaidon Press Ltd
First published in French as
Rien n'est Simple by Éditions Denoël
© 1962 Sempé and Éditions Denoël

ISBN 0 7148 4483 7

A CIP catalogue record for this book is
available from the British Library.

Translated by Anthea Bell
Designed by James Cartledge and
Karen Billingham of etal-design
Printed in China